# Around the World Right Now

Gina Cascone and Bryony Williams Sheppard
Illustrated by Olivia Beckman

PUBLISHED BY SLEEPING BEAR PRESS

There are twenty-four hours in a day;
and in the twenty-four different time zones
all around the world, each
and every one of them is
happening right now.

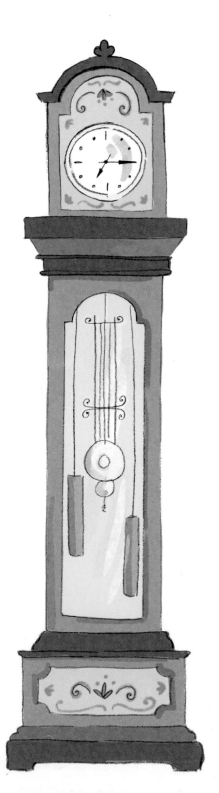

# At six o'clock in the morning . . .

In San Francisco, California, people wake up to the clickety-clack of the cable car on its way to Fisherman's Wharf.

And somewhere in the world . . .

# It's seven o'clock in the morning.

In Santa Fe, New Mexico, an artist sits in front of his easel to paint the early morning sunlight shining down on the beautiful adobe buildings in the Plaza.

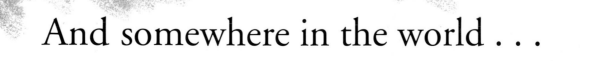

## And somewhere in the world . . .

# It's eight o'clock in the morning.

In New Orleans, Louisiana, people sip coffee with chicory and eat beignets for breakfast at Café Du Monde, near the banks of the mighty Mississippi, as jazz musicians play.

And somewhere in the world . . .

# It's nine o'clock in the morning.

In New York, New York, the streets of Times Square are crowded with people racing to and fro as the workday begins.

And somewhere in the world . . .

# It's ten o'clock in the morning.

In Halifax, Nova Scotia, boats come and go
from Fisherman's Cove taking people out into the
Atlantic Ocean for fishing or whale watching.

And somewhere in the world . . .

# It's eleven o'clock in the morning.

In Rio de Janeiro, Brazil, a girl from Ipanema goes walking on a beach crowded with sunbathers, vendors, and futevolei players to the sounds of bossa nova music.

And somewhere in the world . . .

# It's twelve o'clock, noon.

In the South Sandwich Islands in the southern Atlantic Ocean
nobody is having sandwiches for lunch because nobody lives there except the
volcanoes blowing steady streams of smoke, until the next big eruption.

And somewhere in the world . . .

# It's one o'clock in the afternoon.

In Greenland, an Inuit boy is happily training his first pack of dogs to work together to pull a heavy sled.

## And somewhere in the world . . .

# It's two o'clock in the afternoon.

In London, England, children on a class trip begin queuing up to feed the pelicans in St. James's Park as Big Ben chimes the hour.

And somewhere in the world . . .

# It's three o'clock in the afternoon.

In Rome, Italy, the Eternal City, Italian shopkeepers head home for their afternoon rest as tourists eat gelato and toss three coins into the Trevi fountain.

And somewhere in the world . . .

# It's four o'clock in the afternoon.

In Cape Town, South Africa, children stop skipping rope
to look up at the rainbow that has just appeared over Table Mountain.

And somewhere in the world . . .

# It's five o'clock in the afternoon.

In Madagascar (a large island off the east coast of Africa) along the Avenue of the Baobabs, a playful lemur decides to join a family's picnic.

And somewhere in the world . . .

# It's six o'clock in the evening.

In Dubai, along the Persian Gulf, where it is still too hot to be outside, people gaze from the windows of the top floor of the Burj Khalifa, the tallest building in the world, to look down on the beautiful city in the sand.

And somewhere in the world . . .

# It's seven o'clock in the evening.

In Agra, India, the last visitors of the day take one
more picture before leaving the Taj Mahal.

And somewhere in the world . . .

# It's eight o'clock in the evening.

In Myanmar, Burma, a peaceful yogi practices his poses
as the sun sets over the temples.

And somewhere in the world . . .

# It's nine o'clock at night.

In Bangkok, Thailand, traditional dancers
entertain audiences at the Royal Theatre.

And somewhere in the world . . .

# It's ten o'clock at night.

Near Beijing, China, campers settle down for the night
near the Great Wall of China.

And somewhere in the world . . .

# It's eleven o'clock at night.

In Tokyo, Japan, people take a late night stroll along the Ginza under the blaze of the neon lights.

And somewhere in the world . . .

# It's twelve o'clock, midnight.

In Sydney, Australia, the night watchman locks up the Sydney Opera House after another exciting performance.

SYDNEY OPERA gala

MUSIC

## And somewhere in the world . . .

# It's one o'clock in the morning.

In Vladivostok, Russia, the Trans-Siberian
Railway pulls into the station at the end of its
5,772-mile-long journey from Moscow.

And somewhere in the world . . .

# It's two o'clock in the morning.

At the South Pole Station in Antarctica,
scientists are busy studying the land, wind,
and sky from the coldest place on earth.

## And somewhere in the world . . .

# It's three o'clock in the morning.

Deep in the Pacific Ocean, a baby humpback whale is born.

And somewhere in the world . . .

# It's four o'clock in the morning.

On the North Shore of Oahu, Hawaii, an early morning surfer leaves her house with her board to meet up with the rest of the "Dawn Patrol" to catch the waves before going to work.

And somewhere in the world . . .

# It's five o'clock in the morning.

In Anchorage, Alaska, a lonely moose walks
down a quiet street before the town awakens.

And somewhere the world . . .

It's still six o'clock in the morning
in San Francisco, California.

There are twenty-four hours in a day
and in every minute of every hour
of every day, somewhere in the world,
something wonderful is happening.

# Around the Globe

Our planet is a beautiful sphere traveling through space on its yearlong journey around the sun. We have 5 oceans, 7 seas, 7 continents, and 196 countries, all vibrant with life. Over 7 billion people, speaking more than 6,500 different languages, inhabit this world. We live in different time zones, with different climates, in different kinds of houses. We eat different meals and practice different traditions. We celebrate our differences, as one family, sharing one home . . . Earth.

# Traveling the World

Each country and its people have made wondrous contributions to the quality of life on this planet. Exploring other cultures helps us understand the importance of our differences as well as the value of our universal similarities.

Using a globe or a map, find your own home first. Then mark off the places visited in this book. After learning about your community, travel along with the book, discovering all you can about each location and the remarkable and unique qualities it has to offer. Compare each country's way of life to life in your hometown. Spend some time at your local library or online, gathering information before you move on through the pages. And, of course, feel free to make other stops around the world as well.

# Around the Clock

For thousands of years, human beings have kept track of time. In our early days, it was important to know how many hours of daylight were available to hunt and gather food. Back in 1500 BC, the first clocks were not run by batteries or electricity. Time was calculated by watching the movement of shadows created by the sun. The sundial is so accurate a tool that it was exclusively used until 1400 AD. While rarely seen today, the sundial is the model for our modern clocks.

# Making a Sundial

*(with directions from the National Wildlife Federation)*

1. Poke a hole through the center of a paper plate. Write the number 12 on the edge of the plate. Using a ruler, draw a straight line from the number 12 to the hole.

2. Poke a straw through the hole and carefully slant it toward the line.

3. At noon on a sunny day, take the plate outside. On the ground, turn the plate so that the shadow of the straw falls along the line to the number 12. Fasten the plate to the ground so that it does not move.

4. One hour later, check the position of the shadow along the edge of the plate and write the number 1 on that spot. Continue each hour, predicting the position while checking and marking the actual position.

This activity will help with observation, communication, and prediction skills while having fun learning to tell time the way our earliest ancestors did.

*For Sydney Rose and Ewan Dennis*
*and all the children around the world right now*
—Gina and Bree

*To Dad and Mum, Marina and César*
—Olivia

## Sleeping Bear Press™

2395 South Huron Parkway, Suite 200, Ann Arbor, MI 48104
www.sleepingbearpress.com
© Sleeping Bear Press

Printed and bound in China.
10 9 8 7 6 5 4 3 2 1

Library of Congress Cataloging-in-Publication Data
Names: Cascone, Gina, 1955- author. | Sheppard, Bryony Williams, author. | Beckman, Olivia, illustrator.
Title: Around the world right now / written by Gina Cascone and Bryony Williams Sheppard ; illustrated by Olivia Beckman.
Description: Ann Arbor, MI : Sleeping Bear Press, [2017] | Audience: Age 4-6.
Identifiers: LCCN 2016026771 | ISBN 9781585369768
Subjects: LCSH: Geography—Juvenile literature. | Travel—Juvenile
literature. | Culture—Juvenile literature.
Classification: LCC G175 .C39 2017 | DDC 910.4/1—dc23
LC record available at https://lccn.loc.gov/2016026771